Roadrunner

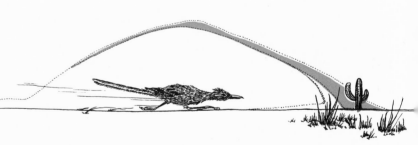

Roadrunner by Naomi John

illustrated by Peter and Virginia Parnall

A UNICORN BOOK

E. P. DUTTON   NEW YORK

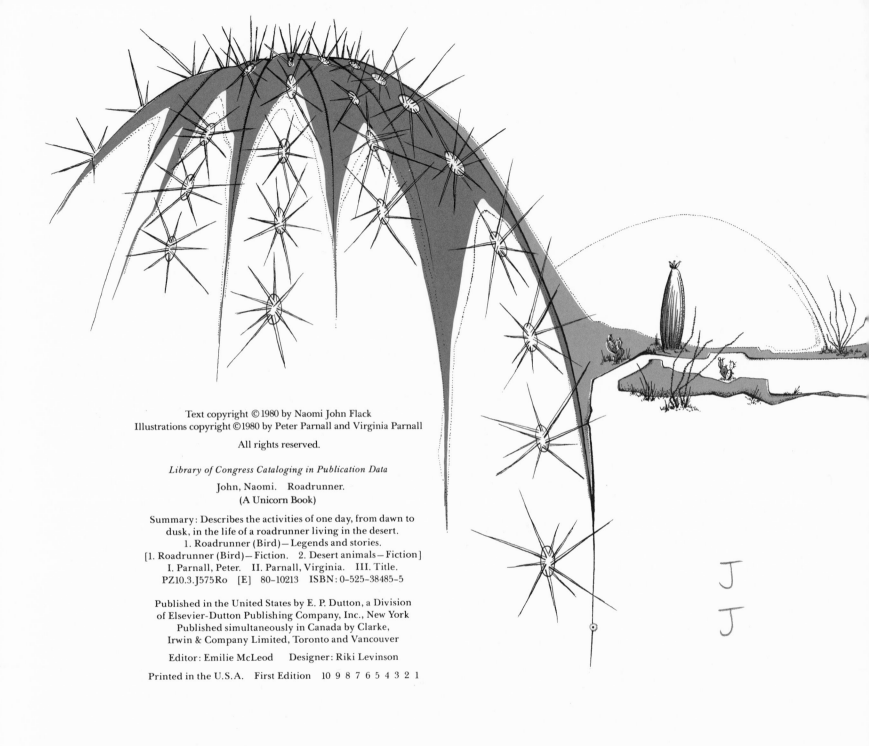

Library of Congress Cataloging in Publication Data

John, Naomi.   Roadrunner.
(A Unicorn Book)

Summary: Describes the activities of one day, from dawn to
dusk, in the life of a roadrunner living in the desert.
1. Roadrunner (Bird)—Legends and stories.
[1. Roadrunner (Bird)—Fiction.   2. Desert animals—Fiction]
I. Parnall, Peter.   II. Parnall, Virginia.   III. Title.
PZ10.3.J575Ro   [E]   80-10213   ISBN: 0-525-38485-5

Published in the United States by E. P. Dutton, a Division
of Elsevier-Dutton Publishing Company, Inc., New York
Published simultaneously in Canada by Clarke,
Irwin & Company Limited, Toronto and Vancouver

Editor: Emilie McLeod   Designer: Riki Levinson

Printed in the U.S.A.   First Edition   10 9 8 7 6 5 4 3 2 1

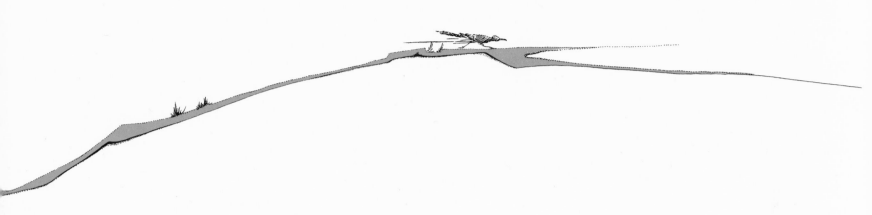

for John

Twice during the night
  the roadrunner awakened.

A coyote, tawny as the desert,
  loped along in the moonlight,
    nose to earth, sniffing.

Near morning, a ring-tailed cat
  slunk by, stalking a pack rat.

Each time, the roadrunner pressed
  himself closer into the notch
    of the saguaro cactus.

When dawn came, the roadrunner
  flew down from his perch,
    fluffed out his feathers,
      and stretched his wings—
        first one, then the other.

He faced the rising sun,
  made a low bow, and sang a small song:
    "Coo-coo-coo-coo."

Then he turned his head
and, with one eye, watched
a red-tailed hawk
slowly circling in the sky.

With the other eye, the roadrunner
looked down at a centipede
on the ground.

He scooped it up, stopped and swallowed,
and ran again.

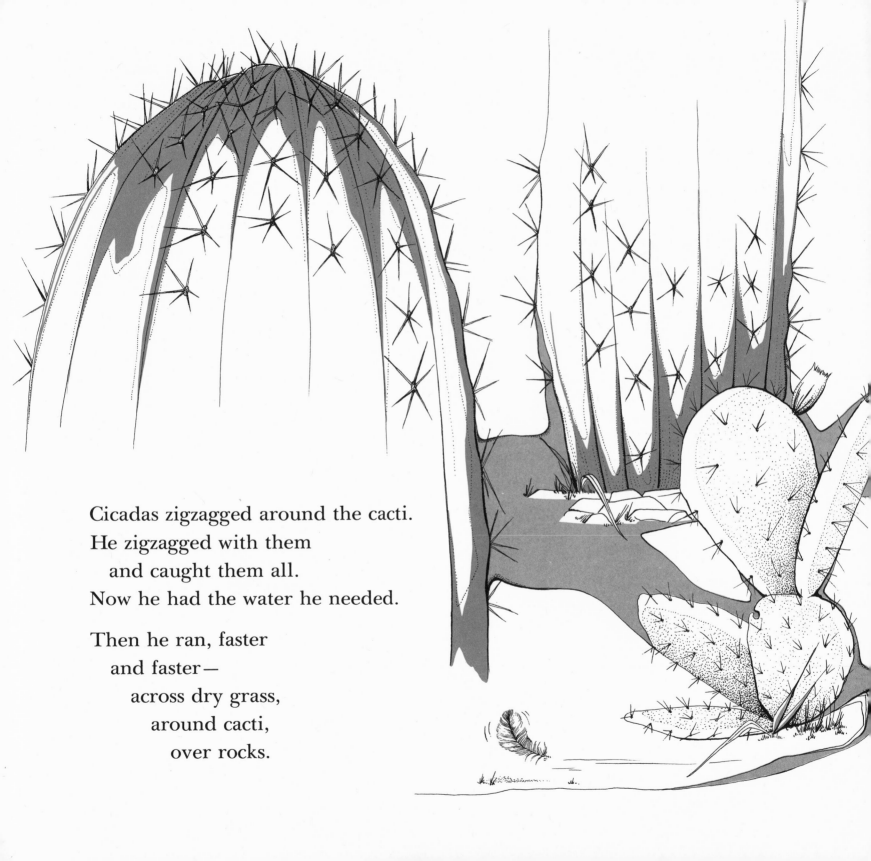

Cicadas zigzagged around the cacti.
He zigzagged with them
  and caught them all.
Now he had the water he needed.

Then he ran, faster
  and faster—
    across dry grass,
      around cacti,
        over rocks.

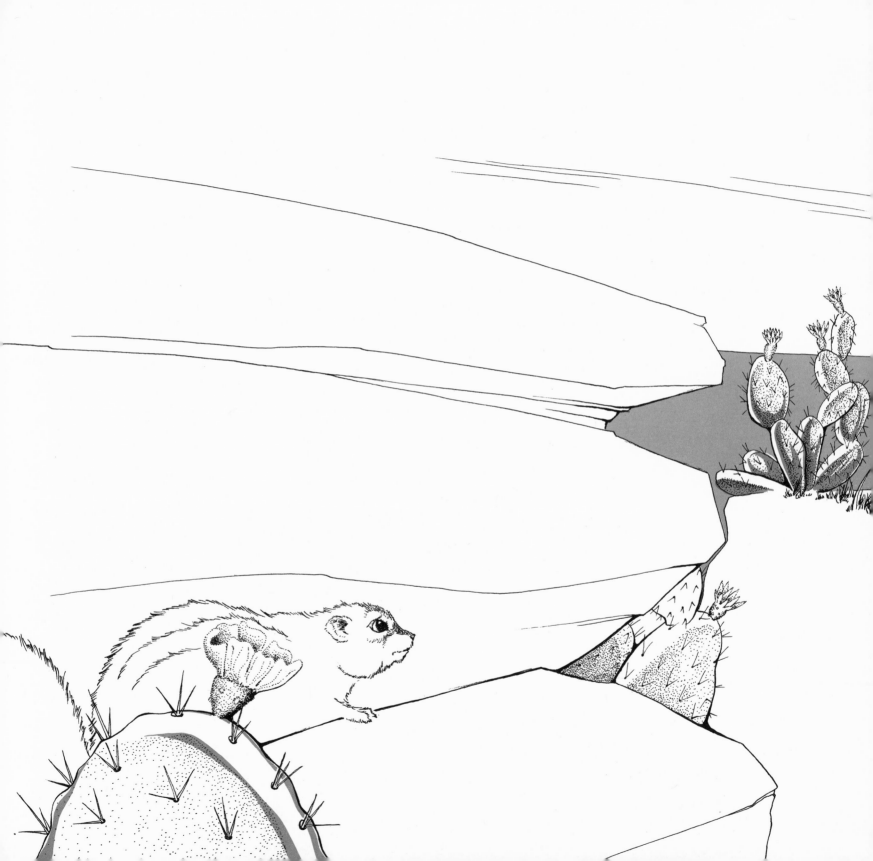

A ground squirrel stood up
   to nibble blossoms of a prickly pear cactus.

The roadrunner came to a screeching halt,
   kicked up a flurry of dust,
      and made a sharp turn.

The ground squirrel slid into a rocky crevice.

The roadrunner ran on.

He found a small lizard sleeping in the sun.
He snatched it, gulped it down,
   and clacked his bill.

A horse and rider came along the desert road.
The roadrunner shot past them at full speed,
   came to a skidding halt,
      and doubled back.

The man called out, "¡Hola! Paisano."

Pacing himself to the gait of the horse,
   the roadrunner ran beside them
      until they turned away from the road.

The sky changed from blue to white.
Heat waves quivered above the earth.
The sun became a white-hot blur,
   burning a hole in the sky.

The roadrunner stopped under a mesquite.
He dusted himself with dirt and settled down
   and dozed.

When the mesquite cast long fingers of shade
   and the air cooled, he ran again.

A small rattlesnake slithered past a rock.

The roadrunner stopped, shuffled his feet,
  fluffed out his feathers,
    swished his tail,
      and stirred up dust.

The snake pulled itself into a tight coil
  and shook its rattles.

The roadrunner raced around the snake.
Suddenly, at mid-step, he changed direction.
The snake, blinded with dust,
  struck empty air—turned, and struck air again.

The roadrunner spread his wings, darted in,
  and pecked the snake's head
    with his long, sharp bill.

Then he circled, reversed, and pecked again.
Finally, he closed in, picked up the limp snake,
   and whacked it on the rock…again, and again,
      and again.
The snake was dead.
Then he ate the snake—slowly.

For a long time he struggled,
   getting the snake down his gullet.
When he finally finished, he clacked his bill
   and stood and stared into the distance.

Then he ran again.
He tried to catch a wren, but
it flew into a hole in a cactus.

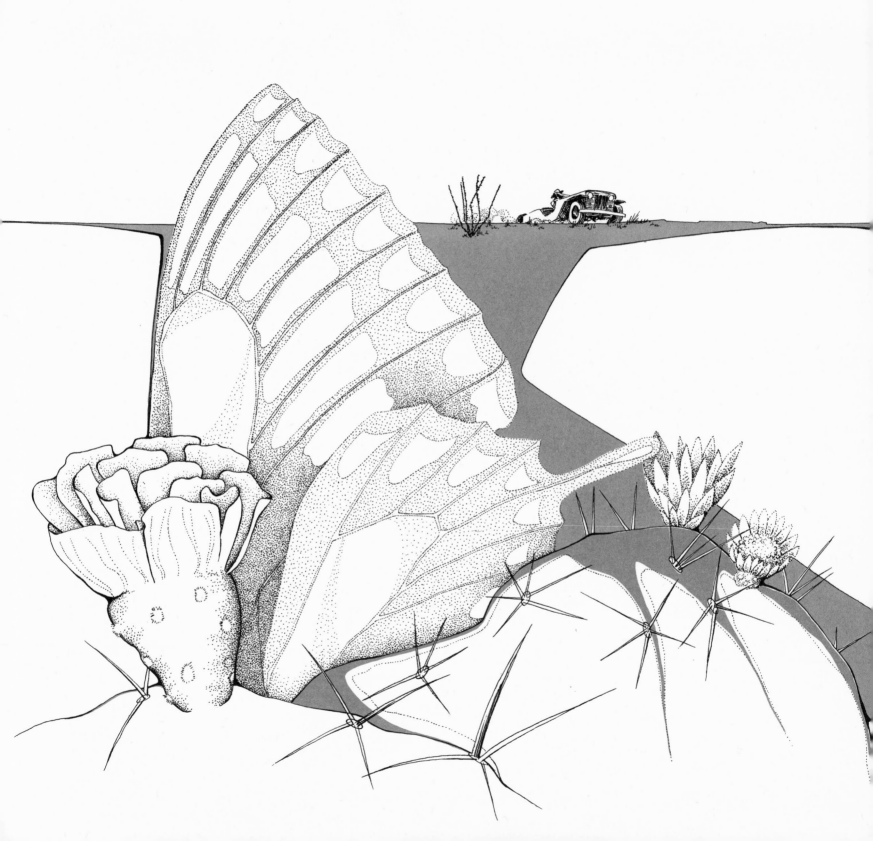

A jeep came jolting down the rough desert road,
    sending up lazy curls of dust behind it.
The roadrunner turned and ran in front of the jeep.

The man in the jeep laughed and called out,
    "Want to race, Big Bird?"

A dog put his head out of the jeep
    and barked excitedly.
The jeep bounced over a rock in the road,
    and the dog tumbled to the ground.

Righting himself, he raced after
    the roadrunner.

Bill, body, and tail
  in a straight line,
    the roadrunner ran
      across the desert.

But the dog ran faster.

When the dog almost reached him,
  the roadrunner braked,
    flung up a shower of dirt,
      and flapped over a pincushion cactus.

The dog skidded
  and rolled into the cactus and howled.

The roadrunner ran on.

He found a nest of quail eggs.

He ate one, piercing the shell with
  his bill.
He rolled a second one from the nest,
  and a shadow fell over him.

The hawk was spiraling downward,
  swiftly,
    talons extended.

The roadrunner left the eggs and ran.

The shadow of the hawk grew sharper.

The roadrunner turned, first one way
  and then another.
The shadow followed him, darkened.

The talons were almost upon him.
The roadrunner slid around a barrel cactus,
  made a complete turnabout,
    and reversed his direction.

When the hawk flew away,
   the roadrunner rested briefly
     under an ocotillo bush.

Then, as the setting sun turned the desert red
   and lengthened the shadows,
     he ran again.
He ran until there was only a glow left
   on the horizon.

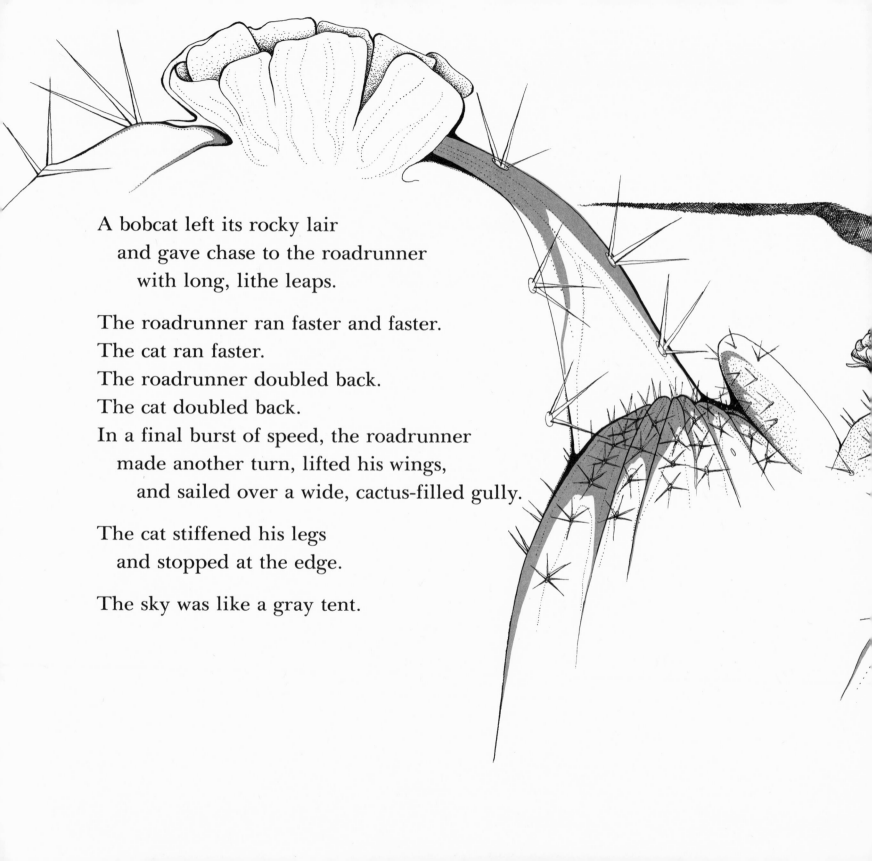

A bobcat left its rocky lair
   and gave chase to the roadrunner
      with long, lithe leaps.

The roadrunner ran faster and faster.
The cat ran faster.
The roadrunner doubled back.
The cat doubled back.
In a final burst of speed, the roadrunner
   made another turn, lifted his wings,
      and sailed over a wide, cactus-filled gully.

The cat stiffened his legs
   and stopped at the edge.

The sky was like a gray tent.

The roadrunner found another saguaro cactus.
He flew to a curve in the lowest arm and settled down.
He smoothed his feathers with his bill and
    sang another small song:
        "Per-r-r-rp...per-r-r-rp...per-r-r-rp."

A coyote howled in the distance.
The roadrunner closed his eyes.